The Art Lesson

For Kathy

Written and illustrated by

Tomie dePaola

Tomie 2001

PAPERSTAR

The Putnam & Grosset Group

For ROSE MULLIGAN,
my fifth grade teacher,
who ALWAYS gave me more
than one piece of paper...
...and, of course,
BEULAH BOWERS, the best
art teacher any child
could have had.

Also, special thanks to
Binney & Smith Inc.
and Crayola crayons. –TdeP

Printed on recycled paper

Copyright © 1989 by Tomie dePaola. All rights reserved.
This book, or parts thereof, may not be reproduced in any form
without permission in writing from the publisher. A PaperStar Book,
published in 199 by The Putnam & Grosset Group, 200 Madison Avenue,
New York, NY 10016. PaperStar is a registered trademark of
The Putnam Berkley Group, Inc. The PaperStar logo is a trademark of
The Putnam Berkley Group, Inc. Originally published in 1978
by G. P. Putnam's Sons. Published simultaneously in Canada.
Printed in the United States of America.
Crayola is a registered trademark of Binney & Smith Inc. Used with permission.

Library of Congress Cataloging-in-Publication Data
dePaola, Tomie. the art lesson/written and illustrated by Tomie de Paola. p. cm..
Summary: Having learned to be creative in drawing pictures at home,
young Tommy is dismayed when he goes to school
and finds the art lesson there much more regimented.
[1. Artists–Fiction   2. Individuality–Fiction.] I. Title.
PZ7.D439Ar 1989[E]–dc19 88-27617 CIP AC
ISBN 0-698-11572-4

Tommy knew he wanted to be an artist when he grew up.
He drew pictures everywhere he went. It was his favorite thing to do.

His friends had favorite things to do, too. Jack collected all kinds of turtles. Herbie made huge cities in his sandbox. Jeannie, Tommy's best friend, could do cartwheels and stand on her head.

But Tommy drew and drew and drew.

His twin cousins, who were already grown up, were in art school learning to be real artists. They told him not to copy and to practice, practice, practice. So, he did.

Tommy put his pictures up on the walls of his half of the bedroom.

His mom put them up all around the house.

His dad took them to the barber shop where he worked.

Tom and Nana, Tommy's Irish grandfather and grandmother, had his pictures in their grocery store.

Nana-Fall-River, his Italian grandmother, put one in a special frame on the table next to the photograph of Aunt Clo in her wedding dress.

Once Tommy took a flashlight and a pencil under the covers and drew pictures on his sheets. But when his mom changed the sheets on Monday and found them, she said, "No more drawing on the sheets, Tommy."

His mom and dad were having a new house built, so Tommy
drew pictures of what it would look like when it was finished.

When the walls were up, one of the carpenters gave Tommy a piece of bright blue chalk.

Tommy took the chalk and drew beautiful pictures all over the unfinished walls.

But, when the painters came, his dad said, "That's it, Tommy. No more drawing on the walls."

Tommy couldn't wait to go to kindergarten. His brother, Joe, told him there was a real art teacher who came to the school to give ART LESSONS!

"When do we have our art lessons?" Tommy asked the kindergarten teacher.

"Oh, you won't have your art lessons until next year," said Miss Bird. "But, we *are* going to paint pictures tomorrow."

It wasn't much fun.

The paint was awful and the paper got all wrinkly. Miss Bird made the paint by pouring different colored powders into different jars and mixing them with water. The paint didn't stick to the paper very well and it cracked.

If it was windy when Tommy carried his picture home, the
paint blew right off the paper.

"At least you get more than one piece of paper in kindergarten,"
his brother, Joe, said. "When the art teacher comes, you only
get one piece."

Tommy knew that the art teacher came to the school every other Wednesday. He could tell she was an artist because she wore a blue smock over her dress and she always carried a big box of thick colored chalks.

Once, Tommy and Jeannie looked at the drawings that were hung up in the hallway. They were done by the first graders.

"Your pictures are much better," Jeannie told Tommy. "Next year when we have real art lessons, you'll be the best one!"

Tommy could hardly wait. He practiced all summer. Then, on his birthday, which was right after school began, his mom and dad gave him a box of sixty-four Crayola crayons. Regular boxes of crayons had red, orange, yellow, green, blue, violet, brown and black. This box had so many other colors: blue-violet, turquoise, red-orange, pink and even gold, silver and copper.

"Class," said Miss Landers, the first-grade teacher, "next month, the art teacher will come to our room, so on Monday instead of Singing, we will practice using our crayons."

On Monday, Tommy brought his sixty-four crayons to school.
Miss Landers was not pleased.

"Everyone must use the same crayons," she said.
"SCHOOL CRAYONS!"

School crayons had only the same old eight colors.

As Miss Landers passed them out to the class, she said,
"These crayons are school property, so do not break them,
peel off the paper, or wear down the points."

"How am I supposed to practice being an artist with
SCHOOL CRAYONS?" Tommy asked Jack and Herbie.

"That's enough, Tommy," Miss Landers said. "And I want
you to take those birthday crayons home with you and
leave them there."

And Joe was right. They only got ONE piece of paper.

Finally, the day of the art lesson came. Tommy could hardly sleep that night.

The next morning, he hid the box of sixty-four crayons under his sweater and went off to school. He was ready!

The classroom door opened and in walked the art teacher. Miss Landers said, "Class, this is Mrs. Bowers, the art teacher. Patty, who is our paper monitor this week, will give out one piece of paper to each of you. And remember, don't ruin it because it is the only piece you'll get. Now, pay attention to Mrs. Bowers."

"Class," Mrs. Bowers began, "because Thanksgiving is not too far away, we will learn to draw a Pilgrim man, a Pilgrim woman and a turkey. Watch carefully and copy me."

Copy? COPY? Tommy knew that *real* artists didn't copy.
This was terrible. This was supposed to be a real art lesson.
He folded his arms and just sat there.

"Now what's the matter?" Miss Landers asked. Tommy looked past her and spoke right to Mrs. Bowers.

"I'm going to be an artist when I grow up and my cousins told me that real artists don't copy. And besides, Miss Landers won't let me use my own sixty-four Crayola crayons."

"Well, well," Mrs. Bowers said. "What are we going to do?"
She turned to Miss Landers and they whispered together. Miss
Landers nodded.

"Now, Tommy," Mrs. Bowers said. "It wouldn't be fair to let
you do something different from the rest of the class.

But, I have an idea. If you draw the Pilgrim man and woman and the turkey, and if there's any time left, I'll give you *another* piece of paper and you can do your own picture with your own crayons. Can you do that?"

"I'll try," Tommy said, with a big smile.

And he did.

And he did.

And he still does.

May 22, 1997.
The day after you
were born —

Dear Emana — I'm not sure
how to spell your name — but welcome
little girl to this beautiful world. Your Grandma
Ellen could not be here when you were
born — so I rushed out to Stillwater and
saw you before you were an hour old —

You are lovely —
With love
Great grandma —
Kitty

DEDICATION

To Connie and her remarkable strength of spirit,
And to the spark in each of us.

ISBN paperback 1-883220-26-2
hardcover 1-883220-25-4

Published by DAWN Publications
14618 Tyler Foote Road
Nevada City, CA 95959
(916) 292-3482

Printed on recycled paper using soy based ink
Printed in Hong Kong

10 9 8 7 6 5 4 3 2

Designed by LeeAnn Brook
Type style is Papyrus

A SPARK IN THE DARK

WRITTEN AND ILLUSTRATED BY
RICHARD TICHNOR AND JENNY SMITH

DAWN Publications

AUTHORS' NOTE

Stories of creation have been told by people everywhere, throughout time. These stories are not only fanciful tales from the past but are also allegories for the present. They are told symbolically so that each person can interpret the meaning in their own way. For example, the star in our story may represent God to some people, or to others, it may symbolize the explosion out of which our universe grew. On a more personal level, the star may symbolize any act of creation, a new burst of growth, or the creative spark within us. There are as many possible interpretations as there are readers.

The details of each creation story are different, reflecting the people who tell it. But if you listen carefully, you will find that all of these stories have similar underlying themes which tell us about ourselves—our place in the universe, our relationship with others, and our inner experience. That these stories are told by people all over the world shows us that inside we are not so different after all.

Through our story about creation we hope to remind people of what we all know but tend to forget in our everyday lives: that we all come from something larger than ourselves, and that we are all related in this way. Our story is also intended to remind people that we are all special, that each of us has the potential to bring light into the world.

This is the story
of a Star in the sky,
of where we all come from
and the answer to "why?"

It's about a blue ball,

a mountain and tree,

a light in our hearts,

and our reason to be.

A long time ago,

when the sky was

still dark...

In a faraway corner

flashed a bright little spark.

It grew into a Star,

way up in the sky.

Since no one was there,

no one asked "why?"

The Star loved the darkness,

it helped it to shine,

but was all by itself for a very long time.

And the Star grew lonely up there in the night,

with nothing to shine on or receive its star light.

So it made
a blue ball,
and spun it
around.
It was pretty
to look at,
but way
too
far
down.

So the Star made a mountain
grow up from the sea,
and said to itself,
"Now it's nearer to me."

But the mountain just sat there,
did nothing at all.

So it put a
green tree
on the
little blue ball.

Now the Star had the water,

the mountain and tree,

but still was not happy —

how could that be?

As the Star looked around and pondered its plight,

it spied down below its reflections of light —

Down on the water they danced and they swam.

The Star had an idea! The Star had a plan...

It took a deep breath,

'til it started to strain,

then starbeams fell down

on the mountain, like rain.

They burst into Beings of bright colored light. They could feel, they could hear, they could see every sight!

They ran, they skipped, they tumbled and played on the mountain and tree that the Star had just made.

And the Star was so happy with what it had done,
it fell asleep in the sky, tired out from the fun.

When day turned to night,
the Star opened its eyes,
to twinkling lights
that filled up the skies.

What happens,

you see...

in each child's heart

glows a piece of the Star,

of which we're all part.

In the sky up above, as each child dreams —
like the water, the darkness reflects their light beams.

While the children all sleep on the blue ball below, their lights twinkle above in a beautiful glow.

The star was delighted,
it sparkled with glee,
surrounded by lights
from within You and Me.

So remember, tonight
as you sleep in your bed,
a light from within
shines over your head.

And that is the story
of a world that began,
with all little children
as part of the plan.

No matter the color,

the shape big or small,

the Star loved them all

on the little blue ball.

About the Authors

A Spark in the Dark was written by Richard and Jenny as a Christmas gift for family members. The story was shaped by their shared interests and experiences. The mythological and symbolic elements were inspired by the writings of Joseph Campbell.

Richard began drawing and painting as a child; he is now an architect. Jenny has a master's degree in consciousness studies and has worked with both children and adults. Together they have shared many adventures: they've lived on Cape Cod; in France; and in a log cabin in the Sierra Nevada Mountains. They currently live at Lake Tahoe in California. *A Spark in the Dark* is their first book.

Acknowledgments

We would like to thank our family and friends for their encouragement and interest. We also appreciate the support and efforts of everyone at Dawn Publications. And a special thanks to Bob, Glenn, and LeeAnn for their openness and guidance throughout the evolution of this book.

Dawn Publications is dedicated to helping people experience a sense of unity and harmony with all life. Each of our products encourages a deeper sensitivity and appreciation for the natural world. For a catalog listing our complete product line, please call (800) 545-7475.